*Dear Susan,
To one of my dear+
loveliest friends.*

Carl

To Jack Daniels, for easing the pain,

and to Naomi, for getting it.

Tens

We met when we were ten. You were bigger than me and you used to bully me daily: slap me, punch me, kick me, and worse. You told me later the choice of whom to bully was between Johnny and I and Johnny was only nine, but we both know why you picked on me, and why I didn't just turn you in. It was love from the moment we met.

One day you tried to kick me in the shins, but I dodged to the side and caught your foot and made you hop while your skirt flew up and everyone in the fifth grade stared at your panties. Your eyes burned daggers at me!

Forty years later, things haven't changed much. You still bullied me and kicked me and when I couldn't take it anymore, I caught your foot up and exposed your truths. Childishness is excusable in ten year olds, not in fifty year olds.

I'm writing this to go back to the beginning, to understand how my pain evolved with you. I don't think this will serve any purpose but to put closure on our last chance, the one golden chance at true love. To throw the last shovel of dirt on a decayed corpse forty years lingering.

I guess you sort of killed it and broke the funeral to boot, you know?

It was an innocent time, 1967 to 1968. The world lay ahead of a scrawny little blond-haired boy. Living where I did, I had the best of both worlds and the worst.

I grew up the son of an immigrant laborer and had friends like me who lived crowded into four room railroad flats. A few blocks further south, there were friends like you who lived in luxury high rises.

Of course, your parents could barely afford the apartment and you really should have been my neighbor in our cold water walk-up, losing heat and even water every Christmas when the super went on vacation and shut things off because he wasn't tipped well enough. There are few more embarrassing sights than a family filling water jugs at the fire hydrant on Christmas morning on the Upper East Side.

I had street smarts and book smarts and because I was smarter than nearly every one around me, I was a freak.

So were you. You were born in California, moved to New York City a few years later, and from what I can see, never truly had a place you can call home. It almost seems like you were always on the run from something. You never had roots. You never committed to one place. One wonders why all the discomfort in simply being in one place, just enjoying who you are.

Your mom was a European "noble" who married beneath herself and your dad spent his entire life trying to fix that for her. Sounds familiar, doesn't it?

We were stuck in a special education class of our own, gifted education. We studied opera and French when the other classes were struggling with basic geometry and English. We were elites and we were treated accordingly. We were even interviewed for a national magazine.

This budding nerdling expected to be beaten up on the streets. The swarthy blue-collar Sicilian kids of my neighborhood resented this little blond boy with the chiseled cheekbones and cowlick – you and Karen used to call me "Woodstock," remember? – but I never expected that in school that I'd be so brutally smacked around by a girl.

I had to lie to my parents and blame Fred so they wouldn't make fun of me.

I tried to avoid you at first, which only infuriated you. So I fought back, even though you had a height, weight, and reach advantage. I didn't give as good as I got, but I battled. I'd antagonize and tease you until you lost it.

Sounds very familiar these days. The child is the mother or father of the woman or man.

I confess, I can understand your frustration in getting my attention: eight boys and sixteen girls meant that this really cute boy with the ocean in his eyes and the sun in his hair was getting a lot of attention.

Like I said, immature behavior for a ten year old is fine. We were only just becoming aware of our sexual identities, just developing our libidos.

I adored you, in that warped way a scared uncertain awkward little boy does.

You were cute. Oh, God, but you were cute! You had this wonderful head of auburn hair almost always in pigtails. Your eyes with shaded rings of green and a tinge of fire-bright orange just by the iris, the same flame I saw when I caught your leg!

And by extension, your heart.

You had this wicked evil smile, like you knew a secret that no one else could know. I look at our class picture and see that smile, now etched for eternity on a small girl mature way beyond her years. I wonder if you were thinking of ways to humiliate me just as the photo was snapped.

Or maybe you were just that abused as a child. It's hard to say.

I make no bones about this: if I could travel back in time, back to our beginning, I would pick my younger self up, sit him on my knee, and explain the future. What will happen, what could happen, and urge him, beg him, to kiss you and say the words to you that have been my privilege to say many times.

"I love you."

And now, my embarrassment to have said all those times.

I wonder how different things would have been if you had just stopped hitting me.

Do you remember performing a play for the Parents' Association? I was the lead and I so wanted you to be opposite me. It didn't happen, of course. Nancy was given the part and we did a fine job.

That must have killed you, knowing I was "romancing" Nancy publicly. You'd never show it, of course, but I do remember that you were a lot more aggressive around that time.

I think it was around this time when you broke your Thermos over my back swinging your lunch box at me. You remember that? Heck, you had to remind me of it.

Those lunchboxes were heavy tin and you swung your arm all the way around because I had been annoying you. You caught me-- POW!-- right across the shoulder blade or goodness knows I'd probably be wheelchair bound.

I think I could hear the crunching of the broken glass as you stomped away.

You had—have-- this horrible temper. You've never really learned to control it or yourself. I guess that's why you have to control everyone and everything around you.

Then there was the spitball fight. I think our regular teacher was out on bereavement leave, and we had a substitute who excused herself from the classroom for a moment.

I don't recall who started it, probably me, but a spitball war broke out in the class. Someone got the bright idea to open the window and pelt passersby.

Naturally, people complained.

The principal came storming in, shouted at us, and after some questioning, we all had notes sent home.

My dad signed mine. Of course he then tattooed my ass with a belt.

I got spanked a lot. Dad was not a small man, either. He was a soldier in the war, a survivor of a near-lethal wound. Shrapnel entered his back and came within millimeters of his heart. He moved to the States and fathered five kids.

Only three survived. One, my brother, was disabled early, felled by meningitis. It was the Fifties and Sixties, so my sister wasn't expected to accomplish much, and besides, men didn't deal with daughters.

Me, I was the surprise, six years later. I was both the star child and my father's last hope, so pain became a constant companion for me. I guess between his frustration with the first four and me being light years ahead of this poor man who could barely speak the language of his adopted country, he lost it and often.

I had dreams as a kid. I wanted to play baseball. I hung out for hours in my "backyard," a concrete patch six feet wide by thirty feet long, surrounded on three sides by the walls of the buildings stretching thirty feet high or more and on the fourth side by an eight-foot high shack. You'd probably mock it, as you mock so many things you do not understand about me, and never bothered to find out.

It was my refuge. I could be an explorer in the airshafts between the buildings. I put up a basketball hoop. And I used to spend hours back there working on my pitching and pitching to myself (using a wall) so I could practice hitting.

It was my Fortress of Solitude. And I became really good. I could focus on the little things that make a great ballplayer.

But my parents said no. Back then, ballplayers worked jobs in the off-season, digging graves and working in offices. This was before free agency. My folks from a backward farm country couldn't have foreseen the golden contracts to come.

They insisted that I focus on my brain, and on school.

So I became really good at school. I pulled grades that were second or third in the class, behind only Jane and sometimes Johnny.

You girls really stuck together and it was interesting to watch the hierarchy develop. There was Liza, Yoko, and Marion at the top of the pecking order, then it was Ann and you and Nancy and Lana and Jane, and then Maggie and Lisa, and then a bunch of girls who were so forgettable that I look at pictures and I still don't know who they were.

Marion later told me that you girls tried to hang out with the boys, but we'd have none of it. It was hard. You were all so much bigger than us and a bit more developed. Hell, Kristin practically had to wear a bra! It was a little intimidating!

You and I were still locked in our love-hate battle through that entire year. I recall we had our desks arranged in a square around the perimeter of the room. I kept dropping my pencil to look up your (among others) skirt.

Even back then, I knew where I belonged. I think I came up once to a paperclip whizzing past my ear.

The walk home from school was a half-mile and took me past the entrance to a busy bridge. Every day, I took my life into my hands dodging cars and trucks and buses.

You turned in the other direction, the rich kids' direction. For all I knew of that life, you could have been chauffeured home on magic carpets.

How different things could have been if your parents hadn't put on airs, and chose to live in an apartment they could afford. I could have carried your books. We could have played together, gotten past the frustration. We could have played house or doctor and expressed our love on a deeper level. But like Tantalus and the water and food, it would always elude us, always that dream of a life with you would remain out of reach.

Fifth grade ended and you moved away. It was that Spring that you broke your thermos on my arm. I don't recall knowing that you were moving away. I think I did. Perhaps I should have kissed you goodbye.

It's a pity you had to leave. Sixth grade was fun.

It was 1968. The Jets, led by Joe Namath, a hero of mine and passing acquaintance later in life, were piling up wins, making the fall a magical time. I begged my parents for a Jets helmet for my birthday. I was shocked that they actually bought it.

A bunch of us, including Mark and his younger brother, began playing football near your old apartment in a cul-de-sac. I discovered that I had a pretty good arm and could call plays, so I took up football. I became really good at it. I had quick feet, quick reflexes and could anticipate moves my opponent would make then fake him out of his socks.

That Christmas I came down with the Hong Kong flu, suffering a 104 degree fever with vomiting. There's a picture of me somewhere cuddled under a quilt with a "Merry Christmas" card all you can see besides the quilt and one hand. I'd not been that sick since I was born dying.

See, mom was Rh negative and I was positive and her blood was both bringing me sustenance and killing me, as her antibodies began tracking down my blood cells and killing them as invaders.

I required a full blood transfusion when I was born to flush the antibodies I retained. I was, in effect, allergic to my own blood.

To this day, I'm convinced this is why am a fighter and a survivor. And I will survive this final blow of yours, dust myself off and give you the ultimate "fuck you, princess."

The Jets won the Super Bowl that January. I was sitting in Tommy's house, wearing my helmet, holding a handmade poster cheering them on.

Tommy had the greatest collection of *Mad* magazines. I learned satire from many an afternoon spent at Tommy's. This is why I'm so easily able to knock you down a peg. You can blame Tommy.

The Knicks began to wind into championship form, and the Mets began their improbable season. Man was about to land on the moon!

It was little boy heaven!

In school, we worked hard. My folks refused to let me join the glee club so while the rest of the class was warming up their pipes, I sat in the room practicing for all the standardized tests to come: reading, math, Iowa skills.

I scored college level reading grades and could handle high school math. We hadn't even studied algebra yet.

You had stopped hitting me, and I excelled beyond anyone's wildest expectations.

Yes, the boys and girls still teased each other. Once, I slapped Lori's arm and she and her sister chased me a block and a half, nearly catching me until I ducked under Tracy's arm and doubled back through traffic. I think Kathy and I may have had a go at it, as well.

The world was my oyster. I was even named captain of the crossing guard, although I was originally elected lieutenant. I can't recall who actually won the election or why they had to drop it, but I was so proud of that blue and silver badge. I may still even have it.

Despite all that, and all my choices for girlfriends, I focused my now-blossoming puppy love on Ann.

Who refused me. I hadn't asked her personally, passing word along the grapevine that I liked her. Her attitude was, "well, let him ask me." Probably the right way to handle that.

Karen, your friend and deep rival for me, was devastated. She kept after me after you left, and I suppose if the year had lasted one more month, she and I might have hooked up. I had noticed her, finally, after Ann turned me down.

It's funny that when we reunited this year, the first two people you went out of your way to mock (besides me, I mean) in your inimitably bitchy style were my wife and Karen.

But then you never handled competition well. You got too wound up, too anxious, and then you'd panic and get frustrated easily. You couldn't commit yourself to a complete win.

And then you would always, always, let your temper get the better of you. I know. I've seen it happen first hand throughout your life.

My first kiss came that year, too. Marion held a birthday party and we played Spin The Bottle. My spin landed on Kathy. Or maybe hers on me.

It was...squishy. We didn't know about tongues, so we pressed our lips together. I think she cradled my jaws in her hands. We stayed like that for a while, like in the movies.

It was nothing like our first kiss to come, you and me.

Twenties

Stan and I walked into the bar that late summer night. It must have been 1978 or 1979, because it was shortly after that when Stan and I shared an apartment. I'm thinking it was 1978 because we hadn't even really talked about that.

I agreed to go as Stan's wingman. There was this really hot girl at this bar that he couldn't shake loose from her friend. I figured I owed him. I'd stolen a few of his girlfriends, like

Robin. I could fall on my sword for him this one time.

Stan's first mistake was not telling me which girl he was interested in. I'm not sure it would have made a difference.

We walked in and if memory serves, the crowd, mingling and loud, parted and Stan immediately saw the girls.

The friend, as it turned out the fat chick, was sitting down. She was cute but the blond girl standing next to her was spectacular. The bar was dark, but even so you could see she had "it."

Stan introduced us, and he and I went to get drinks from the bar. The girls were still in the same place when we came back, the blond hottie standing against a pillar, her friend sitting on the half wall separating the tables from the bar.

We handed them their drinks. Again, Stan's bad luck came into play. He led the way back, which meant he stood further from the hot girl than I did. This let him look her in the eye to talk, but left me right next to her.

I don't recall if I started or she did, but we began rubbing up against each other. First, it was arms and shoulders, then hips. The blond sat down, or I did. All I remember is over the course of the next hours, as the conversation amongst the four of us drifted among the detritus of small talk, the blond and I were turning each other on, rubbing thighs and knees and groins.

We kept glancing at each other. She was hot. I was hot.

Because it was a Thursday, around midnight Stan realized he had to get home. He had to be at work by ten. So did I, even earlier in fact.

The blond was in college. I should not have been but I was. After breezing through elementary and junior high schools, in high school I was thrown in with kids my own level and I struggled just to pull Bs.

In college, I discovered freedom. No one took attendance, no one checked homework. I discovered pinball and bars that served any college kid simply because he was in college, never mind that he was only 16.

And girls. I finally discovered girls.

That was 1974. School fell by the wayside. What should have been four years was extended. And extended. I was graduated in 1990, sixteen years later. My own bad, although my dad's heart attack forced me to work full time. The silver lining was my jobs all had tuition reimbursement.

But the blond, she could have been a few years younger than me. Drinking age was eighteen and I'm sure she was of age.

The blond and I walked out. She lived a few blocks east, by the river. I offered to walk her home.

We held hands. We stopped in the dark of the night on the sidewalk and kissed and groped and grinded.

That first kiss was like opening bottled lightning. It had all the electricity and excitement of a porn convention in Vegas at Christmas. I tingled from my toes to my already thinning hair and my eyes popped open because I thought someone had substituted an electric eel for her mouth.

It was like we had been kissing for decades and she knew my mouth better than I did.

We broke the kiss and her eyes remained shut, a beatific smile serenely taped across her lips. I could almost watch her swallow the taste of our kiss.

She suggested we take a walk by the river and sit on a bench overlooking the water, to "talk."

We sat on the first bench we could find and "talked." She practically climbed up on my lap before I sat down, the way a cat jumps into your lap. And we kissed.

And kissed. And kissed. And teased each other, hands remaining discreetly above fabric. Well, most of the time. It was amazing, hotter than hot, the way the movies always portray it when you find "her", the one, the love at first sight.

There was that electricity that made this sultry night steam and boil over. We laughed and kissed and laughed and breathed, both admitting there was more than a flame here, more than a fire.

Oh, we chatted! She was kicked out of a Jesuit college and was now attending a municipal college. I told her the summation of my life in between smacks and sucks of our kissing. I doubt she paid much attention to the details. I know I wasn't.

Finally, I looked at my watch. It was 2:30, and I really needed to get some sleep. I walked her back to her building. We kissed goodnight, our tongues mingling and tugging at each other, caressing and stroking.

I asked for her number and she borrowed a pen and paper from the doorman, quickly jotting down her name and number.

I didn't look at it, but folded it and stuck it in my jeans pocket, never taking my eyes off her. I was too starry-eyed and tired to notice her eyes, her green, green eyes.

I turned and floated out the door, drifting the mile home with a grin on my face. I got about two-thirds of the way there when I decided I had to look at the number and the name in her own handwriting. I couldn't believe how energized, how…in love?…I was.

The name. I caught my breath. Even the unusual spelling.

It was you. It had to be you.

I very nearly picked up the payphone outside the hospital I was walking past to call you until I remembered how late, or rather early, it was.

Likely the phone rang in your parent's room too.

I got home, got undressed and got into bed. I tried to sleep and eventually the adrenaline wore off and I fought my libido for sleep.

I hurried to work later that morning, and took your number out. It was early and you had actually written two numbers down: home and office. Your dad ran an office on 57th Street and you worked there helping him.

My hands shook from exhaustion and excitement and extra caffeine. I dialed, twice. I screwed up the first one. Your receptionist picked up, and I asked for you.

"She's not in yet. May I take a message?"

"Yes. Would you please tell her I called," and gave her my number, but then added, "I need you to ask her a question: can you ask her what elementary school she went to, please"

"I'm sorry…would you repeat that, please?"

You called just minutes later. I have to admit I wasn't 100% certain if you were who I thought you were, so I was a bit scared when your voice was on the line. You mentioned the school. I mentioned the teachers we shared. And then I mentioned my name.

My other name. The one you would have known me by, not the one I took as I grew up.

You went silent, and then burst out laughing. You realized the monumental joke God played on us, but you also knew what I knew. It was hours after we met…re-met?…and we were deeply in love. Fifth grade came into crystal clear perspective. We knew each other better than any lovers could. We were childhood enemies!

Your parents were taking you to the theatre later, but you said you'd like to pick me up for a bite afterwards and to talk.

It must have been past eleven when you swung by my building after *Evita*. You were all dressed up. We walked to your apartment and I met your folks.

They seemed nice. Your mom seemed very happy for us, for you. She even told you *sotto voce* not to worry about your dad, she'd keep him occupied while we got reacquainted.

All four of us had a snack together and some wine, and your parents excused themselves for bed as we stood in the kitchen. And then we kissed.

We did that a lot, even in our fifties. I guess we loved each other a little, huh?

We rolled the television from the living room to your bedroom, closed the door and alternately made love and watched TV. And napped.

You felt good in my arms, but you always have. Your tight body, lithe and supple, your breasts were firm, nipples round and urgent. We burned together with slow soft flames.

Entering the wet folds of you was like taking a trip to Heaven flying first class. And your eyes, those gorgeous eyes, burned with that passion you used to have hitting me, that orange halo of lust that I saw in fifth grade when I grabbed your foot, exposing your panties.

Only here, there were no panties. There was you and me and finally, us. We were. I was where I belonged, where I had always belonged. Where I have always belonged, by your side, within your heart, your mind, your body and soul. In your eyes.

I woke up early the next morning. You were spooned up against me, your tight ass nestling my already-rigid cock, my arms wrapped around you.

I pulled your hair back from your ear and slid the tip of my tongue along its outer folds, pressing my body against yours. My shaft sawed back and forth over your cunt lips like the bow of a violin. You roused from a light sleep, paused, realized what was happening and smiled the most-- maybe the only-- truly contented smile I've ever seen from you.

I lifted your right leg and draped it over my hip, reached in and began to stroke your clit with tiny tight circles against your pubes. You turned your face upwards. Our tongues met in the millimeters of air between our mouths and wrestled there, my tongue stroking yours. You captured mine with your lips and sucked it like it was a cock.

With this, your legs spread wide and I plunged into you, all eleven inches to the hilt. We rocked back and forth in tandem. Coupled. Paired. United.

And when we came, it was not with the histrionics of two panthers like the previous night, but with soft butterfly moans and the gentle shudders of lovers.

We were.

I rolled out of bed around six, got dressed and walked home.

Kids have such boundless energy. Now, after six or seven go-rounds, I'd either be dead or it would be next Thursday.

I walked in the door and my mother was waiting in the kitchen. She wanted to know who the whore was.

Considering this was the first night I'd slept away from home without letting her know where I was, as offended as I was by her words I understood her rage. She was probably mortally scared of her angel being corrupted.

Compassion. I can see points of view without agreeing or judging them.

She was probably up most of the night waiting for either my key in the door or the cops calling her to identify my body. I didn't answer her. I needed some sleep.

I called you later and we chatted, and I asked you out. You had plans for that night. So did I. I went out with her. You know, the woman who later went on to be my wife. We saw a movie, she talked about grad school, and I rode out and walked her to her door. We kissed and said goodnight. All the while, you were on my mind.

I would have broken my date, you know. All you had to do was ask, just say you'd make yourself available for me. History would have changed for want of some self-awareness.

And that's pretty much how things went after that. When we could, which was often, we saw each other and when we were together, we shared a love that Shakespeare could not describe for all the sonnets in the universe. We could have been inseparable, but you had other priorities, friends with whom I had no connections and your interminable rugby games, the ones you stood on the sidelines cheering.

And you <u>never</u> fucking invited me to come along.

There were good times, to be sure, and I remember those most of all, better than the bad.

Like the time I was playing football in the park and I came home to you all hot and sweaty, and you stuck me in the shower and scrubbed my back.

And then turned me around, squatted down and urged my cock to stiffness, taking it in your mouth and hands under the spray of the shower, bobbing back and forth on your haunches.

You sucked me hard, harder than I could remember having it, stood up and turned around and grabbed the faucet. Your ass was firm and wet, and I spread your lips with my thumbs. The intensity was electrifying as I pierced your hot twat and immediately slid all the way in because there was no friction, none at all.

We nearly drained the building of hot water! We spent hours under that spray, collapsed into a wet wrinkled pool of passion on the floor.

If only these times had been the only kinds of times we shared, we would have been perfect. For some reason, you didn't want to go there.

So I dated. I dated her and a couple of others. We had no exclusivity agreement save the exclusion of me in your life. We still spent time together, lots of it. Your parents bought us dinner one night and I still remember your dad smacking my hand at the table with chopsticks for some transgression of manners.

Rude. But funny.

There was this significant part of your life that I would never be part of, and I knew it, and I knew you preferred it that way. That's the compartmentalizing bit of you, the non-committal acquisitive bit that strings people along like so much popcorn garland, or those glittering beads horny teenage boys give their girlfriends for every blow job.

I was in love with you, and this continual rejection broke me. We started fighting, often. At first, we fought about dumb stuff. I'd need a shower, but you'd be in the bathroom, or what movie to see, or how to get you and your bad knee up a flight of stairs, or music.

Then it started getting more serious. We'd fight about spending more time together, or my hunch you were dating someone else…hunches are *nasty* things, you know. They usually are wrong, unless you find clear evidence to back them up.

We'd fight about the future when we barely had the present.

Looking back, it seems oddly poignant that the closer we got to making a life together, the harder you fought and the faster you ran. There's this anxious dichotomy about you that I don't think all the Xanax in the world would have calmed you down enough to make us happen.

You started pressuring me, but for what? I couldn't afford my own place and you couldn't really contribute.

I wonder how different things would have been if you had just stopped hitting me. If you had taken a breath and said our safe word, "lunchbox," and looked at the truth. After all, it was you who controlled things, you who put us in a shiny metal box in your bedroom.

I couldn't hit back, of course. I towered over you and in the ten years' absence, I learned I was physically and emotionally capable of killing someone.

I was fifteen. My friend Artie and I had a crush on a girl named Lisa. He was jealous of me. He was a wrestler and one day, like two elk, we squared off. I had speed and reach, while Artie had power.

He came charging in waist-high and I stepped aside and grabbed his head and rammed it into a parking meter.

Artie lay there, stunned. His eyes shut and I could see he was out cold. I hoped he was only unconscious. I knelt next to him, trying to revive him. A shopkeeper hurried over with some water that he splashed Artie's face with.

He woke and staggered to his feet. A couple of friends helped him walk home.

It was pure reflex, but somewhere inside, I had the urge and it slipped out a little. So when you'd slap or punch me, I swallowed hard.

Victims of violence, particularly as children, particularly if there's been emotional humiliation as well, tend to be violent. It's probably a testament to my intellect and emotional training that no one's been hurt around me, save Artie.

So, when ten years after you used to bully me constantly, you were still being aggressive and even violent, it was harder than you know to swallow hard and take it.

More painful, though, was how you would ridicule and denigrate me in front of our friends, insulting and mocking me. I have a pretty abrasive tongue, but you have carborundum compared to my sand paper. Because we were fighting, I didn't want to mock you and have you take something the wrong way.

And I loved you. I didn't want to hurt you. I've loved you with all my heart and all my soul for all these years, and I didn't want to be the cause of pain.

It's funny, looking back across the seas of time, to see how much I really did love you. You say it was reciprocated, but your words do not jibe with your actions and any excuse--youth, freedom, anger--is just an excuse.

You've never really shown me much love. I'm not convinced you can ever give love to anyone, really. You've never really sacrificed anything for us, that much I can be sure of: never given anything up and you've always insisted that I must.

Still, we had fun. I remember how your friends freaked out when I walked in with an auburn-haired chick one night because you hadn't told them you dyed your hair and it makes me laugh to hear how Susan nearly punched me in the mouth until you went back the next morning for a rugby game and everyone realized it had been you.

And the sex: the role-playing, the kitchen floor, the shower. Your bed with the crosstown buses idling on the corner under your window, a few stories down. Rolling the TV in was foreplay for us.

There was one time when we were fighting about something stupid…I think it was my Dad's birthday the next day and I couldn't see you.

We went at it like cats and dogs until I looked in your eyes and saw the fire, and I pinned you against the wall, tore off your panties and lifted you up high by your legs, impaling you on me. We screamed at the top of our lungs simultaneously and left a puddle by my feet. And laughed hysterically.

We had love of some kind. I just wish I could figure out what.

I smile when I think about wearing your dad's clothes because mine were all wet from the rain, and I looked like a gay Parisian mime in his

French cut T shirt with the purple and black stripes.

And I even have "awwww" moments when I think about carrying you on my back to the movies because your knee hurt.

I suppose there must have been some love there. And I'll even be magnanimous to say that for you, you gave a lot of love.

But something was still missing.

Do you remember the night you were so high on mescaline I had to come pick you up and walk you across town? The mica chips in the concrete were blinding you under the street lights. And that night and the next day, you mocked me because I expressed my concern that you put yourself at that kind of risk, and my anger that you dumped the responsibility of your safety on my shoulders.

It wasn't long after that night that we parted. I don't remember, or even really care about, the exact dynamic of our parting. If you say it was my fault, I accept that. We broke up ultimately because it stopped being about us as a couple but about us as individuals.

And yes, the next night, she and I went to see the Laserium show that I bought us tickets for. The tickets you basically told me to shove up my ass.

Did you imagine I would apologize for what you did to me?

After we split, the world was once again open to me. The Rangers played for the Cup the next Spring, and I became friends with many of the players: Duguay, Esposito, Fotiu, J.D. We hung out in the same bars, dated the same girls, had the same friends.

And then I married a few years later. I married her. You would have mocked me, but you know what? As bad as the marriage was even from the get-go, she stuck around. She didn't have priorities that didn't include me. As disconnected as we were, it beat being harassed and rejected daily. She was willing to look past my flaws to see the good, decent, caring man I am.

I was willing to look past yours to see the love that I thought was there.

I went to therapy for my marriage when things got tough. Not your kind, not the "here's a prescription, now get out" kind, but the kind that challenged me to look at who I really am, to take a good long look at myself.

I took up acting, as well, because in acting I am able to be myself uncensored but safely in character.

Naked, but veiled. I learned a lot about myself, mostly the power of the truth and how to communicate that. I would be honest with everyone in my life.

Not cruelly, not brutally, but honest.

So she and I went to couples therapy and individual therapy and we had a baby and she and I worked, sweated, argued, loved and hated each other until one day a few years later we looked at each other and realized it wasn't working.

We didn't get divorced. We separated a few times, but drifted back together. Sometimes the separations lasted years. We had a child that we created and we <u>owed</u> fealty to that. You mock us, but then you never had a baby of your own.

We didn't stick together out of some misguided sense of love, but for the purely practical reason that when you create a life, you create obligation.

Since you never had a baby, what could you possibly know? You rented them from other women as you stole their husbands! You could return them when they or the marriage broke!

Fuck, it wasn't even a long term lease! You dumped out of both marriages in less than ten years combined!

I committed to my life. You flitted around like a butterfly.

And what did you do after we parted? Appeared nude in a girlie magazine with your 60 year old "noble" mom performing a quasi-lesbian spread. Yes, I suppose it was art, but what the hell were you thinking?

Maybe you weren't. It wouldn't be the first time or the last.

Fifties

As I sat there on Facebook back in early March of this year, looking at your email, part of me said, "Do not respond."

It was a flash. A "hunch," if you will, since hunches matter so much to you.

I guess it was a hunch *I* should have listened to.

I looked at your picture. You were wearing your little Dutch Boy wig of highlighted auburn hair. You looked like an old French hooker past her retirement. I assume that was the look you were going for?

I convinced myself…it wasn't hard…that thirty years was more than enough time to let bygones be bygones, to say hi, and to renew acquaintances with you. After all, I had forgiven and moved on. Hell, I thought I had forgotten you. All I knew, all I could remember, was how much I loved you, not how much it hurt to love you.

I looked up your profile. You had some intriguing experiences and adventures.

You lived on the other coast. I felt the distance would help us heal old wounds and find closure. God help me, I had no intention of falling for you again, but perhaps the distance made it easier to both idealize you, us, and to keep you at arm's length. Falling in love would be easy since in no way could we ever act on this.

Little did I account for our passions. I revealed my heart and my truths to you. I spoke plainly and honestly about what I had been up to for the past thirty years, married and children and jobs. And it was hard to remember the mechanics of our split, although many of the details seemed clear in your head. Thirty years will do that to me, to good memories and bad.

I told you who I married and you told me I was nuts. Maybe I was. Maybe I did it to spite you. Maybe I did it to spite my parents. Maybe she was the ultimate "fuck off" to the world.

I don't know that I will ever understand why I married her, but I loved her once upon a time. Not as much as I loved you, but then she's never hurt me as much as you did in the brief periods we shared.

In truth, as I told you early on in our most recent reunion, while you were not on my mind, you were in my head. As we talked more, I realized you had always been there, looking over my shoulder, even if I never really acknowledged you.

I guess the difference between you and I is you claim not to hold grudges, to move on quickly, while I allow myself the freedom to process the pain and what I feel, to integrate my emotions and then to dismiss the pain.

Pain leaves sharp memories. As one who has suffered many pains at the hands of many people I've loved and trusted (parents to lovers to children), this I can assure you. By dealing with it in the now, I don't leave it to fester and sabotage my dealings with new people, people who didn't hurt me, people who didn't rob me blind or cheat on me. It even allows me to truly forgive.

And if their actions hark back to earlier pain, I can speak my mind.

I do remember earlier this year writing you an apology for the hurt and pain I caused you all those years ago. Apologies are awesome forms of love. In giving one, you give up your defenses and admit your humanity. In accepting one, you gain a piece of the divine but you also achieve some completeness, a sense of a being made whole.

I'm still waiting for an apology back. Now two.

I'll even offer this one last apology to you: for the horrid things I said to you in the heat of our most current and final breakup and breakdown, for the name-calling and false accusations, the vile characterizations and the raging, I am sorry.

Any defense I could offer would only be an excuse, like I did it out of panic, or that you struck the first hundred blows against me before I finally retaliated. What's done is done, and however wrong or nasty or abusive you were, I should not have stooped to the level I did.

Despite your immature foot-stamping and ridiculing and irrational exaggerations based on hunches and paranoia, and your outright fabrications, you are a human, an adult woman, and so deserved more mature handling.

Again, I am sorry.

How did we get here, dear? Less than a month ago as I write this, I was lying in your arms, holding you tightly and swearing my oath to come to you for the rest of our lives.

And now I'm just swearing at you.

We quickly fell in love again. The passion we had at ten, at twenty, carried into our fifties, after we'd both led lives bereft of that passion except those fleeting moments we were able to steal them from someone, we were ready for each other.

Finally!

We were both so in love we decided to write a book about the chance meeting back in the 70s and our current reunion. This book.

How do you like it so far?

We talked about the distance. We talked about my marriage. We talked about how to be together: do I move there, or you here? Do you give up your job of many months, or mine of many years?

You were skeptical. So was I. We decided to let this take however long it takes: a year, a year and a half. I wanted to be fair to my wife, who had just lost her mom and was losing her job. I hated the thought of hurting someone who put up with me for all these years. Maybe it wasn't the best marriage, hell, it wasn't even a good one, but it was two people who were in a circumstance together and she deserved some consideration.

We both agreed that this should take time. You were sensitive to my needs, sensitive to my sensitivities and sensibilities. I loved you for it, more than I had ever loved you before. We would spend the next fifty years together making up for the first fifty we spent apart. What was one more year? That's what you said.

We talked about sneaking visits in to pass the time and to reconnect. You mentioned you might come to the city in late April and could spare a day or two to see me. This excited me. The thought of us again, together, in the flesh, made my month and a half.

You came here and we drove out to Montauk,
nervous and excited, making small talk,
catching each other up face-to-face on our lives:
your first two marriages, how I graduated after
sixteen years of college, where you had worked,
where I had worked, friends. I was giddy. My
mouth hurt from smiling.

We reminisced. And kissed. Our first kiss in the
car when I picked you up more than made up for
all the lost kisses we gave to the wrong people
but the kisses that followed at stop lights and
stop signs and even while moving wiped all
those away. The years melted. The calendar
flew backwards. We were kids again.

We arrived at the resort. Despite the early
Spring, the day was bright and sunny and hot,
except right by the ocean where our room was.
It was foggy, even misty, but that happens on
Long Island in April.

We checked in, dropped our bags in the room,
and almost immediately made love for the first
time in thirty years.

It was heaven! It was heaven to feel your skin. It was heaven to kiss you. When you pressed me to my back and climbed into bed next to me, and took my rigid long thick cock in your hands and looked up at me, the years melted away, and I saw that twenty year old girl with the evil smile and evil intent.

And you bent your head and parted your lips and your mouth was like syrup as you sucked me. I grabbed your hair-- well, wig-- and pressed you gently down deeper. I rubbed my thigh against your pussy, urging you on.

When I could no longer bear the thought of not fucking you, I threw you on your back. You were so ready for me, wet and slick. Given our later discussions, this should have been a surprise, but given our earlier encounters, it was not. You were hot. I was hot.

I put your legs around my hips, and you eagerly pressed them open as I slowly pierced your hot twat and penetrated you inch by inch for what seemed like hours until I was fully embraced by your folds of lust.

We made love tenderly at first, as if we were both covered with electric quills. I was stroking your hair and kissing your mouth, your eyes, your nose, your forehead, giggling and laughing with you, but finally, I poised up on my hands and began to piston inside you in earnest. I could feel the cum bubbling in my balls and swelling my shaft, and you, you were already spasming in wave after wave of orgasm.

I came, hard, roaring your name, and my entire essence, my being as well as my cum, penetrated into you. Even you noticed how hard I came. I wanted to be in you, to be you, to see the world and feel the world and hear the world as you do, and in that instant, in that orgasm, I could. We were one. Thirty years apart and not one beat missed!

We were.

We spent most of that day and night doing precisely that, laying in each other's arms and making love, and talking. We walked on the beach, hand in hand, watching the water crash on the sand.

We made plans to hold a class reunion, a 40th anniversary, when you returned to NYC in July. I had already located several old classmates, including Marion and Ann. I suggested we announce our intentions as a couple at that party, making the party all about us. You smiled and hugged me tightly. It would mean the world to us, and to them, to know we were.

We talked about our situation. You had clearly made some decisions about us, how a year was too long (Oh, how I agreed with that!), and perhaps we should be together by the end of the year. Wouldn't it be great to spend Christmas together?

Yes. Yes! YES! Eagerly, my heart leapt at this. I had my misgivings…after all, it's Christmas and then there's the whole family thing and breaking hearts, but in the end, I said yes, without reservation.

We talked about my daughter and how she'd have a place to stay in LA so she could visit, and how my cat could come out and stay with us and your two cats. You asked me if any of this scared me, and I said yes.

I was worried I'd end up homeless on Venice Beach with my cat, but this meant something to me, something very important: A happy Christmas in a happy family with you.

And then it dawned on me that we hadn't talked at all about you moving here. But you made your case: I should move out there, a change of scenery after fifty years.

Besides, you have been moving all your life and you just got this job a few months ago and it paid really well, and you weren't ready to uproot your life and move again. You had done it enough. I had never done it. It seemed fair. Stupid me and my blindspot the size of a bus.

And even though I was all but ready to pack right then after this weekend we spent, I said,

"Let me come see for myself." And we made plans for a visit to your neck of the woods.

We talked about what I needed to accomplish: find a lawyer to decide where to get my divorce (here or there), find a place to live in the interim, quit my job. But we agreed, all of that, ALL of it, could wait until we settled on where to live. We did agree to set some interim goals, like telling my wife that I was unhappy with my life as it was, to put her on notice that things would end shortly.

And we made love. Again. The third time in four hours, and by far not our last.

I drove you home the following day to your parents' apartment on the Upper East Side, the same apartment we spent all that time together in the 1970s. We had some champagne with them, to toast our renewal.

We walked to the bench we first fell in love on, thirty years earlier. It was late afternoon. The sun was descending.

We sat and held hands and watched the river, nearly wordless except for the occasional observation about a bird or boat. We kissed.

It felt right. It felt complete. It felt real. It felt like the past thirty years were just a series of bad dreams, like you had been there beside me the whole way, and woke me up when they got really scary.

It felt like we were, and we would never not be. We imagined walking to this bench every year and sitting, even if it meant two wheelchairs. We vowed we would be married at that very bench.

We gazed at each other. I cried softly when you cried, choking back my tears. I believed the end of all my fruitless searches could be found within your eyes. We held each other close, your shoulder buried under my arm, head upon my chest, our hands clasped in my lap.

Soon, too soon, it was time for me to go back to the life I would soon leave: my rental life.

We walked back to your parents' building, and I kissed you goodbye. Your flight was the next day.

You called me that morning at work and asked to see me for lunch and we met. I reaffirmed my love for you, over and over, and my intent to be with you, over and over, and how happy and giddy you made me.

And to confirm our plans to spend our lives together, first on your coast. After I checked it all out, of course.

Over the ensuing weeks, we were on cloud nine. We realized we still had it, the love we so clearly felt for each other. We counted the days down to my trip like it was a world tour of our favorite band. We talked, maybe not nightly or daily, but more than a few times a week, and constantly emailed and texted each other.

We were inseparable.

Each night, despite sharing my bed in name only with another woman, I felt closer to you. I would fall asleep remembering the feel of your back against my chest, your ass against my thighs. I'd pretend my hand was draped around you, cupping your breast, stroking your nipple.

When I felt really alone, I would find a private place, usually the bathroom, and stroke myself hard looking at your picture, then recreate in my head one of our encounters, like the one outdoors on the stairs to the beach when you squatted and took me in your mouth, furiously bobbing your head up and down as you grabbed my hips and pulled me tightly to you, then stood up, turned around and bent over, displaying yourself, holding the railing for balance from the force of my thrusts.

Sometimes I'd wake up really early and find you had left me a voicemail during the night. You, too, needed the release so you would call to hear my voice as you came, your monstrous "back massager" on high, over and over again.

It was hard sometimes thinking about you out at the local salsa bar or on your friends' boat or at their houses. I'd be sitting home texting you, or calling you, trying not to interrupt your life but wanting to reach out.

And I did, practically every night. I wanted to be close to you, to be yours, and to make sure you knew it.

Oh sure, we had a few dust-ups, mostly dealing with loneliness. You found it hard to believe that I could spend night after night going to sleep in the same bed as a woman I did not love. I would reassure you as best I could that you could park a car in the space between us, but it only helped a little. I felt that my actions towards you would have to convince you.

And you accused me of hitting on our friends, whom I was working tirelessly to arrange our reunion with. You were coming, and I was moving heaven and earth to try to get things in place to make it perfect for my baby and in the course of things, we all grew closer, trying to catch up on forty years.

And I kept at it. I kept trying to please you. I kept my bargain and told my wife that I was not happy, and even added that I was going to make wholesale changes to my life across the board.

I could not have hinted anymore clearly! We agreed it would be a mistake to say anything that would get her to consult a lawyer before I had actually filed for divorce or at least moved out of that house so that was how I left it.

Finally, the day arrived to come visit you, just days after my wife got her layoff notice. You had raised a minor stink about the time of day I was arriving, near midnight, but I had booked the flights thinking I might work the day I was coming. When I realized I probably should give work a miss, it was too late for me to move my flight up.

But I tried, and I would have gladly spent even a few more hours with you.

It was amazing to see LA, a city I hadn't been in for over twenty years, through your eyes. We drove around, we talked, we laughed, we ate.

And made love. Oh, but did we make love. We made love in your bed and your bed felt like home. It was home, red walls, hummingbird and all.

Do you remember how that silly red drape you have over your bed collapsed on my head and you took a picture of me? I was lying there, naked, this diaphanous curtain across my face looking for all the world like a cheap drag version of a harem girl.

I remember laying in your arms, and talking about us. I had made the decision long before I came out that we would be in your place, because you told me time and again that you wanted your man to put your needs first.

I wanted to be that man for you. I wanted to put you on the pedestal you so richly deserved after me, after your ex-husbands Mike, and Jose, after God knows how many others, and keep your needs uppermost. I wanted to protect you the way no one else had stepped up to do, to comfort you when things got bad, when your folks passed on, to pull your hair back when you threw up. To honor and cherish you.

In exchange, all I wanted was to have the right to come to you with my dignity intact and my head held high, that I completed my life as it was doing the best that I could by everybody. To be honored and cherished for the man I had become, not what you thought I should be.

"Should" is the most dangerous word in the English language. "Should" implies expectation and judgment and who wants to be judgmental at our age?

I wanted to hold to my principles of not doing harm by anybody. How could I truly put you first if I didn't have the benchmark of me second? How could I really know I was there for you if I was not there for me?

You can't go through life without hurting people. That's the nature of life. Sometimes it's a zero-sum game, and one person wins which means another loses. But that's life, and you deal with it.

However, you don't have to cause harm. You can choose to not deliberately make someone else's life harder than it already is, even if the goal is to make your life better.

Hurt them? Yes. But harm them? Cause them unnecessary pain?

No one has that right. My wife and I were in pain, and leaving would ease our pain, yes, but there's no point in getting there by violently shredding her into bits. We shared the pain, so it was up to me to mitigate it.

And then you dropped the bombshell: I needed to move out as soon as possible in the summer.

I held my breath. The moment of truth had arrived. If I was going to back out now, this would be that time. The odd pervasive gloom that shrouded LA each morning seemed particularly thick this day. Perhaps that was an omen.

I said, "I'll tell her by September 1 that I'm leaving and leave that day." You smiled and held me close as your head lay on my chest. I could refuse you nothing. You held me.

I wanted to be with you. It meant waiting ten weeks, ten stinking, lousy, short little weeks, in which period you would have visited Mexico, had your parents stay over, have come to NYC again for the reunion (and you wanted to experiment with working out of the NY office), and I would have had my vacation, booked and paid for long before we met.

Not a whole lot of time to plan things, but it would have happened. I swore it, promised it, and would make it so. I was committed to you, to this, to us. I would move heaven and earth when the time came.

We were happy. We made love. We lay in the cool air of your bedroom, the hummingbird chirping away outside like a squeaky rocking chair on meth.

A frozen moment in time. Perhaps it was our last truly in love. You had, I knew, set the price for our love. The cost to me would be dear, but I comforted myself with the knowledge I could still accomplish this on my psychic terms somehow. The balance would be off, but acceptable. It was a price I was prepared to pay.

I left that weekend and flew back to the city, more determined than ever to do this. After all, I could ride my bike 350 days out of the year and ride along a beach for miles and miles. I could get healthy again, and have my life's love by my side to deflect the slings and arrows. Together. With love, cherishing each other truly until death did us part.

Who wouldn't want that?

Your parents flew in to see you the day I left. We missed each other by a few hours. You and I spoke frequently that week, basking in the afterglow of our nuclear fires.

You prepared to go to Mexico later that week, to reacquaint with an old travel buddy of yours. You were leaving Friday, returning the following Tuesday, and to make sure I was not out of touch, you purchased an international cell plan.

Friday came and you took off, texting me as the doors closed. I thought to myself that I needed to let you get settled in at the hotel and to catch up with Richard over drinks and dinner.

According to you, he was gay, so I wasn't worried about the two of you. Friday evening came and went, and I did not hear from you. I figured you would text me when you landed and if you hadn't, it was because either you were tired and still settling in, or the calling plan had failed.

I had intended to call you Saturday morning, but I woke up to a nasty, sarcastic, cutting text from you, about how I was so silent even though you had taken pains to make sure I could get in touch with you.

I tried to explain my sensitivity to your needs, about how after jet lag and dragging a suitcase through customs and then catching up with your friend, I figured you'd need a break, and I apologized for guessing wrong.

And then we chatted and talked and texted and emailed constantly until you came back and beyond.

One day! That Friday comes back to haunt me soon enough. But we fell back into our routine of speaking daily and emailing and texting and things seemed fine.

It was the following Saturday afternoon, two weeks after my visit, and I was lonely and alone, so I called you to say hi. The conversation turned into a review and referendum on how I've not kept my promises to you, promises like finding a lawyer or moving out…moving out?...and how you suspect I won't be moving out.

Huh? You gave me basically a week since your return, a week in which I had to actually work at my job, and then which priority took priority? Getting a lawyer? Moving out? Telling my wife? Give notice to my job and see if I could somehow arrange to work there one week a month, flying back as I needed to?

This arrangement of ours went from giving me the space and time I needed to being a panic-stricken jump-through-hoops effort to placate you!

Is it any wonder I balked? I wasn't jumping high enough to keep up with the hoop you kept raising!

But I started anyway. I asked around, even spoke to our old friend Marion, and got a referral to a pretty decent lawyer who had a west coast office. I had the appointment set up. I did that Tuesday, and the appointment was the following week.

I spoke with my wife that Wednesday, and told her I was leaving shortly. I did it making my heart as cold as possible, but I did it. I didn't specify a date because I thought you and I would discuss that when you came for the reunion in three weeks.

I had planned to surprise you when you came here in late July. We'd be in the hotel room, a bottle of champagne on ice. I'd sit you down, and open the champagne and toast us.

I would take your hand and look you in the eye, and say "I have some things I need to tell you." I'd tell you the advice the lawyer gave me, and how I told my wife, and how much it hurt and how scared I was.

After, when the tears of joy stopped and when I stopped sobbing because of how horrible I felt…after all, if I couldn't confide my pain and fears to my soul mate, who could I tell?...we'd make love, sweet tender love.

And we'd be free to be together.

That was Wednesday night. I decided that was how I would tell you. You had been unusually distant and quiet all day, a couple of emails and one or two texts but no phone calls, despite the voicemail I left you. You were going out with friends that night. I presume you were telling the truth.

Thursday, you dumped me. Over tickets to an art exhibit. Remember? You had sent me an email earlier that week mentioning this exhibit that was going to be put on after I got there, in late September and that you'd get tickets whether I'd say yes or not, since you could probably convince a friend to come along. Thursday comes along, and you start bullying me over not responding to the email from just the other night.

Tickets. You were getting anyway. You didn't say, "Why don't you tell me if I should get these?" or even "Gee, I'd like to see this, what do you think?"

You said, "I'm getting them." I figured I had, you know, a few weeks and many other more pressing issues on my plate than to answer a "question" we both already knew the answer to.

It seemed pointless to keep the appointment with the lawyer now.

I called you, and you started haranguing me. First, you suggested we take a brief vacation from each other, say, three weeks, and then when you came here, pick it up again. This was "take the pressure off us both".

Pressure? Darling, the only pressure was the stuff you were putting out! But I sensed something more was going on, so I said no. I asked what this was all about, and you went back to our conversation that Saturday past, about how I hadn't made those plans or even consulted with a urologist to get a Viagra prescription.

I guess five times a night wasn't enough, but there it was. We did talk about Viagra because I felt I wasn't achieving a full erection and we both know I'm pretty well-hung, ten inches when I'm hard, more when I'm overheated. But that was hardly a priority and I had already spoken to my cardiologist. That's how I knew I needed to see a urologist, and the cardiologist's appointment was just that past Tuesday! It was only <u>THURSDAY</u>!!!

And besides, it didn't seem to stop us from having balls-to-the-wall sex, pretty much at your request.

We started yelling at each other and it was then that you told me, you couldn't put your finger on it, but you had a "hunch" that I was not being honest and that I'd leave you in the lurch and not move out. This was why you suggested a three week vacation and--

I shouted at you. I wondered if my hunch about you and someone else was true, since we were "hunching up" now. You were offended, big time. Understandably. I said it deliberately to antagonize you. Remember the missed kick?

I hung up the phone in disbelief. I couldn't hear anymore of what you were saying, anyway. I was in shock. Was I actually hearing you break up with me?

You kept turning up the pressure on me and then were shocked that I exploded. Kind of irrational, don't you think?

Why didn't you just hold my head in a bucket of water for a couple of minutes and then express shock that I violently spasmed to try to get air? Same difference!

You called me several times after that but I let it go to voicemail. To this day I haven't listened to those. I deleted them and…

I couldn't speak. I could barely breathe. My life's plans had just disintegrated in a flash of smoke and lightning. It was all I could do to hold myself together to send you texts and emails, over and over again, getting angrier and angrier at each happenstance. I didn't have to think to text or email, and I certainly didn't have to listen to you argue with your inane inarticulate bullshit, and I could blurt out my feelings a little at a time without your incessant self-aggrandizing interruptions.

I went onto Facebook and apparently, you had already told your friends we were through. I can't imagine where you found the time, between emailing and texting me back and arranging a date out of spite with the man whose number you said you threw away!

Indeed, it was odd that you never threw his number out. How pedestrian this daughter of Euro "nobility" turns out to be!

I was devastated. Worse, I saw that you were accusing me to *my* friends, to *our* friends, of being a flat-out liar. As you see, it's easy to prove a lie (your back door man), but I couldn't possibly prove a truth to someone who so clearly had unilaterally decided I was lying, or had a different agenda than ours.

A liar? I was honest with you from the day we started speaking and you called me a liar. You looked me in the eye when I promised to be with you, and you had to see the truth of my words there, yet you called me a liar.

And as it turned out, it was you who was lying. You were calling up that old boyfriend all along, the number you promised you'd throw away.

Well, that shattered any image I had of you. Of us. Any illusion was gone.

Hundreds

John Milton wrote that "The childhood shews the man, As morning shews the day," an assertion that the unity of the child's personality manifests in the adult, as the day follows the dawn.

Wordsworth said it, "The child is the father of the man." What we learn to do as children stays with us all our lives unless we purposely change them and even then regression lingers in the background.

You are a bully. Hell, you even threatened to call my wife when I refused to cower in the corner when you broke it off!

You are a bully and were a bully and you haven't gotten enough help to get you past that part of you. You're tempestuous and angry and you rage and you have deep deep insecurities as to your worth. This is how you ask for attention, this is what you mistake for emotion. Rage is not a real emotion, it is your fears and your defensiveness about your insecurities and weaknesses.

Oddly, I found that attractive about you. I mistook it for commitment and love when it was focused on stealing me from my wife. I wonder what would have happened if you had the commitment to follow through with that?

You broke up with me because you had a "hunch" that I was not being honest, not committed to our plans.

Your first husband left his wife and children within two weeks of fucking you because he said he "couldn't live a lie." How terribly romantic! It must have made you feel incredible.

So how many women was he screwing around with behind your back within weeks of the move, including the one he ultimately shacked up with and left you for in Wisconsin, after moving you out west to LA from Chicago? All along, you had no "hunch" until your marriage was the cheat and the cheat was his love, and apparently, he had no problems with living with all *those* lies! He took you for a weak sucker.

Your second husband pandered to and pedestaled you over and over with his greasy Latin American lust. Again, how terribly romantic! How flattering!

Until he sucked all your money dry of you and forced you into bankruptcy, and then walked out on you. And you had no "hunch" until it was too late and you were circling the drain. Apparently, he too saw no problem in taking you for a weak-minded fool.

Me? I was just honest with you all the time. I wanted us to be together and I tried to move heaven and earth, but I wanted to do right by my family. You know, mother-in-law freshly dead, wife's job freshly lost, trying to get my daughter through community college and back to a university to get her degree? No harming unnecessarily? Remember principles?

Me, you have a "hunch" about. Me, I get taken for the fool.

It was never a matter of compromise for you. It was always about your deadlines. At first, I admit, you tried to be sensitive to my needs, even offering to see if you could bring your job here to New York, and giving us a year to settle down into a life together.

And then it came down to an ultimatum of moving there within just a few weeks! Leaving in July, the following month!

As you kept saying those last weeks, it was all for "my own good," right? The word "should" came up often. I should move out in July, it was for my own good?

When I balked, you became abusive. You'd mock me for everything from my early bedtime to my erectile "dysfunction" to how I'd slurp my drink and you even threatened to break up with me if I wore my baseball cap backwards while we were out shooting pictures! I thought you were kidding but considering the bullshit excuses you finally came up with, maybe I should have taken that more seriously and caught the next flight home.

How cruel and insensitive you could be! And in the end, you just got crueler. You just got more insensitive and less caring.

When you have a relationship, even a dying one, you try hard to think about the other person's needs. You said it yourself, you wanted to be put first in your lover's eyes. I was prepared to do that. I wanted to make you feel the best you've ever felt about your life. I wanted to roll the clock back forty years and have a do over.

But in truth, you wanted to be first <u>and</u> <u>only</u>. You told me you wanted someone to put your needs first and not only was I willing to do it, I was DOING IT! But you stopped caring about my needs.

You pressurized this relationship and as you pressurized it you inflated yourself at the cost of us as a couple. I became less and less important as you puffed yourself up to be more and more self-important.

My big mistake in all this was in not insisting you earn the privilege of being put first, ahead of everyone else, especially ahead of me.

See, you claim that Mike and Jose walked out, but here's the thing: there's a common element in both of those relationships, and it's you.

Mike pretended to put you first and somehow, you screwed that up, because he quickly put you last. I have my suspicions why.

And Jose pretended to put you first for his own deceptive reasons, but no one told you to finance him until you went to the poorhouse. He was the broke son of a fabulously wealthy family…what did that tell you???

I should have put up a fight. I should have demanded we compromise. I should have spoken up for my needs. Instead, I gave my heart, without question or pause, to someone who had not earned it, and didn't deserve it.

You accused me of manipulating our friends, but I told the truth about what happened and all I wanted was my privacy to deal with my pain. YOU decided to take all this public and lie about it. You dragged them all into this and humiliated me and them in the process.

It wasn't enough that, at the very moment we could have grabbed happiness you dumped me. No, you had to go pour poison into the ears of people who bore neither of us any ill will, had no reason to dislike or mistrust me until you told your half-lies and paranoid fantasies.

You had to isolate me like an infectious disease and turn a squabble into a full-fledged ware, forcing people to choose sides and becoming agitated and infuriated, raging, if they chose to stay out of it.

I guess I had a romanticized image of those friends, too. People I would have thought to be reasonable, to think beyond the *MTV*-style campaigning you engaged in. I suppose I should thank you for showing me that they are as superficial as the average person.

It's funny how we cling to these idealized portraits of people who were friends long ago. We idolize them or demonize them. It's what we did with each other…certainly I discounted your very deep personality flaws…and I suppose it's what we did with our friends and our friends did with us.

We want to believe things do not change, that people from that innocent age remain encased in the ice of innocence and naivete even tho we should know better. People age, mature, and face the slings and arrows of life. We all grow thicker skins, some thicker than others.

The point to keep in mind is we all made it this far, and so all deserve the honor of making up our own minds. I would have liked to continue that journey with those friends, but you saw an opening to exploit their fear and ignorance before I had the chance to establish my reputation in our newly-reunited group as an honorable, decent and compassionate man.

That was inexcusable, but you also amply demonstrated the romantic flaw in my reminiscences.

So thanks.

I wanted to be alone with my pain and rejection but in the end, you had to break the farewell to control even that. So I fought back the only way I could, with facts and truths and openness and leaving my heart out on the table for everyone to see. I live with my truth. You cannot.

Damn, but that pissed you off, because you had no way of controlling that. And now my private pain is in print for the entire world to read.

So how do you like me now?

You committed to what you knew was a mistake by breaking us up, making good on your ultimatums, and then tried to bluff your way through. You thought you'd break me for good and were willing to give up on our relationship to do it, to get this one last inch of change out of me.

You came up with more excuses to get out of this relationship than George Bush had to get into Iraq. You couldn't come up with a big factual incident, like me philandering on you, or me stealing you blind, like your husbands did.

So you had to make up stuff that wasn't there. I don't know precisely why you ended this, but you gave me the following excuses:

- I hadn't responded to your request with respect to the art exhibit.

- I hadn't spoken to a lawyer (that you knew of).
- I hadn't found a place to live.
- I hadn't rented a van to move my stuff out.
- I hadn't quit my job.
- I hadn't asked for a divorce (that you knew of).
- I hadn't gotten Viagra.

All within ONE STINKING WEEK! Oh…and I hadn't called that one day you were in Mexico.

All of which you could have had a definitive answer to by September 1. Instead, you rushed to judgment, took a flying leap into the swimming pool of assumption and it was empty.

Maybe if you had kids of your own flesh and blood, you'd have learned patience. Your excuse was that you married men who had them already but no one forced you into those marriages at gunpoint. You could easily have found a man who wanted more children and had them. There was a time when you were hot enough.

This was the easy way out, however. It was more convenient and you didn't have to worry about your boobs sagging or losing the baby weight.

You chose these men as your husbands, and it is our choices that speak volumes about us. You wanted the authority to control the kids without the responsibility for the outcome. You couldn't commit to the actual act of loving your child no matter what, of raising a kid even if that kid needed discipline. You'd leave that to the blood parents, I'm sure. You *wanted* to be "Rent-A-Mom"!

Authority without responsibility; It's how you handled me. It's how you've handled your work life, it's how you've handled everything. Control, accept no responsibility, then bail the hell out.

Wait ten weeks, and our bliss is yours. You couldn't even wait that long. You needed to assuage your anxiety right then, right there. And I finally had enough. You couldn't even give me that much of your heart, some patience and a lack of judging until you had cause to judge!

You told me I needed help. I don't need help. It's not me who takes Xanax and still has anxiety attacks and insomnia! I sleep like a little baby, remember?

I put everything on the line for us: my life, my family, my home.

I did that, because I loved you fully and believed we could create something beautiful.

You put nothing of yourself into this. You would have sacrificed nothing. All I ever needed you to put in was your faith and your trust.

Trust comes from the head. Faith from the heart. And when trust conflicts with faith, you should let faith take over. There are powers greater at work in the world than your small conscious mind can comprehend.

It is wrong to mistake faith with trust. Trust is mental. Trust is weighing the evidence and consciously agreeing to someone else's behavior. I don't blame you for not trusting me, with all that your husbands took out of you. Hell, even your dad would lie through his teeth about "the next big deal" and how he'd pay you back and make it all up to you! No wonder you couldn't trust me.

But, that's where faith comes in.

Faith is from the heart. Faith is from the other 90% of our minds which looks beyond the superficial to see the emotional and subconscious make up. You can earn trust, but you must give faith.

Faith is believing in someone. You can have faith in someone even if your trust is shaky, but it's very hard to trust someone you don't have faith in. And you have no faith.

Faith is planting a seed in the ground and waiting, nuturing it with water and sun. You don't dig the seed up to inspect it daily. You'll kill it! You'll put too much pressure on its growth mechanism. You let it be, and it grows.

I <u>deserved</u> your faith. My entire life speaks of my determination, my commitment, my courage.

It took me sixteen years to get my degree, but I got it.

I was in a miserable marriage for 25 years, but I stuck it out to help raise my daughter.

I had a daughter and raised her, and while we may not see eye to eye, she is my daughter, not one I have to share with two other blood parents.

I was in a boring job because eleven years ago, I realized I would need a steady income and more important, to put money away for retirement.

You, you have no kids, the longest you've worked at a job is two years, and your two marriages lasted, what, a grand total of ten years? To boot, you kept your options open going into this arrangement.

How could you plan on spending fifty years with me, when you hadn't spent five years in a committed relationship with anyone? Not husband, not child, not lover; truly, not even parents?

Because you put nothing in, because you have no faith, because you weren't truly committed, your paranoia took over. Your head began to believe there would be payback down the road. Just like with Mike. Just like with Jose.

Of course, with them, you actually put something in. Me? Eh. Not so much.

So in your mind, you began to create these "lies" you accused me of, and as the time grew closer for us to be together, my "lies" became bigger.

For love to work, it involves commitment, and commitment requires...no, it demands...an act of faith.

It demands us to look past details to see the truth. We can question that faith, but unilaterally rejecting it means we never had that love in the first place.

I understand how you were hurt badly in both your marriages. I get that. But there's an old saying that 180 degrees from wrong is still wrong, and as you were constantly pointing out to me about my past that you weren't my wife, I am not Mike and I am not Jose! I deserved the benefit of the doubt!

So there it is: you had no skin in the game, so you never truly loved me. You believed you did, and maybe in your heart you did, but you could never truly fully commit because in your head, you cannot trust.

Not because you couldn't believe me. I've established that I was nothing but honest and giving towards you. I've established there is no one on the planet who works harder towards achieving his goals.

You couldn't believe in yourself. So you panicked and saw ghosts. Put it this way, and I'm looking at this from your point of view now: you could have given this ten weeks and gotten the greatest reward of your entire life, with a small chance you'd be hurt.

That's a risk I would have been willing to take. In fact, it was a risk I did take, risking it all for my god-given right to spend the rest of my life with the love of my life.

I am a black hole. You live on the surface with your ghosts.

Psychic space being a finite element if you look in two dimensions, part of the reason you end up in conflict with others is that your sprawl ends up butting against their sprawl, because each of you is trying to get more sprawl. More. More. More.

I'd wager you are always busy doing, well, *something*: Running out to meet friends, working too hard at a job, jetting off to the next vacation. You need the trappings of a "good life", the condo on the beach, the car, fine wines.

You expand sideways because you can't know there's a depth to life, too.

I call people like you, "Flatlanders". In the guise of "expanding yourself," adding sides (to extend the metaphor), you gain no third dimension. You buy this trinket or that souvenir and proudly display them on your shelves to boast of your travels.

You claim understanding of the world around you, but in truth, this is a false logic. For how can you truly relate to the world if you do not relate to yourself? How can you understand someone else and have compassion for their plight if you don't understand yourself and extend that compassion to yourself?

How can you love if you have no love to give?

As I wrote earlier, love is a commitment, and commitments always demand faith. You can only have faith by delving deep into those parts of you that lie covered in darkness, shrouded by the sprawl of your flatlandedness.

Faith is not based on logic or hunches. Indeed, faith is that thing that keeps us tied to what we love when "evidence" suggests it might be time to let go.

I put "evidence" in quotes because none of us can ever really know a truth outside of ourselves. Our eyes deceive us. Our ears hear distant noises that emanate from within us.

Our minds lie to us for...what? Fear? Our protection? Freud was not far off, I fear, when he spoke of the id, the ego, and the superego. Many people you'll meet have a champion superego, but no id. You do not, and don't mistake your recently-reclaimed (thanks to me) libido as an "id." It's not.

Well, that's not completely true. That id shows up in the weirdest ways and those are the behaviors I look at and wonder what the hell were you thinking? Like ending a relationship because it's going too fucking well???

Faith comes from belief. Faith is a never-ending well to draw from.

I am a black hole.

Spending my adult life extending my self-knowledge, I have been able to give love completely.

Love does not necessarily mean another person at all times. One can love oneself, for example, or find love in the smallest acts of kindness and in the roughest, bleakest landscape, in the prettiest poem, or in teaching someone else.

I express this love through my art: my photography, my acting and performing, and especially my writing. By opening my heart to what goes on around me, by drinking in from the fountain of the world, I can absorb that which I see and express how it affects me.

This is something that Flatlanders never get: it's not about seeing the temples at Angkor Wat or the pyramids or Mount Everest, taking a snapshot, buying a trinket, and bragging about it later, maybe saying how you "soaked up" the local culture with a beer and some local cuisine at a *boîte*.

It's about how these affect you. I probably have fewer pictures of more places in the world that I've been than anyone else. And I'd wager I have a deeper understanding of anyplace I've been than a million other tourists.

Do you remember that house on a high cliff, was it in San Pedro? We both took pictures of it.

You probably centered on the house, and maybe you got enough of the cliff to allow for the precarious position of the building.

I took that same picture and focused on the cliff: the striations of layers of history building, year after year, one on top of the other, the roots breaking out into the air, the grass overhanging the lip.

Oh, I included the house, to show it as the burden the cliff must bear until it can no longer bear it, to highlight the foolish transient nature of people who build on land that is ultimately destined to fall.

To highlight the utter shallow lunacy of Flatlanders.

I took that picture that way because I understand the precarious nature of life, how tomorrow, we might all be gone. Or more to the point, how tomorrow I might be gone.

So I want to leave a piece of me in these places. Many people talk about leaving their heart, but for me, I've shredded little bits of my soul and left them behind. Places don't steal my heart. I steal places' hearts and record them for eternity.

I am a black hole. I leave a small footprint on the surface, but once you've peeked into the abyss, you realize there's a lot more down there than up here.

The trouble with Flatlanders is they insist on painting on the surface what they want me to be, to define me somehow. But you cannot define that which you cannot understand.

And then you got frustrated that I no longer fit the definition you gave me in the first place.

I am a being, not a doing. I don't worry that I've held the same job for eleven years, because while I don't enjoy it much, I know that it's comfortable for me, and as many places as I've worked, this is pretty sweet and stable. I looked at my life and realized I had nothing put away for retirement-- a realization you've only just come to at age 50! -- so I vowed I would stay at this place and put something away.

It's time to move on, true. It's liberating to know I will be free soon.

No thanks to you. I had that decision made already on my time and on my schedule.

You jump jobs every other year and believe you are improving your lot, but you collect nothing but a paycheck and a too-long resume. Like a child with french fries, you are grabbing for the next one before you're finished chewing the first one. You make no real commitment to them and it shows. You take no real responsibility to work with you, and it shows.

Further, I understand that my discomfort at work has to do with boredom, the terrible mind draining tedium of having conquered all I can on this employment.

My faith tells me this. I am enough, and my needs beyond the space to explore my space are few. I don't need to be "seen" in a hot exotic salsa restaurant with friends who I can only truly stand when I'm drunk, but my influence is felt in those places none the less.

I am a black hole. By knowing myself, I know everything I encounter. No, I might not know every single fact about everything...although most people will swear I do...but I have a deep comprehension of the truth of it.

So tell me again, what is it exactly that you put into this relationship? Time? Energy, perhaps? A cross-continental flight to get laid? Hosting me for four days, to get laid? And nothing, nothing else.

Oh. And a spare earring from half a set that you lost the match to and you probably gave me that to mark your territory. I tossed that in the toilet after a bout of intense diarrhea. I thought that was poetic.

Look, I don't deny that, deep down inside there is some love and that on some level you recognize that.

I've laid in your arms. I've cried on your shoulder.

Odd that you hadn't cried. Not once.

And I've felt this little girl that you are, deep down, reach out to hold me. I've felt the good inside you.

It's funny. I've talked more about me, more about my life, my dreams, my hopes, my feelings in this painfully public book than in all the hours of conversations you monopolized.

Hours wasted talking about you. Talking about your anxieties about me, or your job, or your trips, or your drugs, or especially my marriage.

All totaled up, I probably spent weeks on the phone or in e-mails putting out this fire or that one for you, busting my ass to reassure you I was really going to be there for you. I never got to talk much about my past or how I got to survive this crazy changing world.

And that is why I wrote this: maybe, somehow, you will read it and recognize who you are (I've taken great pains to change the major details), and more, what you've done. Maybe you'll understand there's a greater world inside you than you give yourself credit for, if you just move that fucking self-important self-image out of the way.

The love you gave was stingy. It was self-centered. You weren't in love with me as much as in love with the idea of being in love with me, the prize of the fifth grade girls. This is the ultimate form of self-love, of treating love as if it was a prize or an addiction.

You loved the feeling of being in love and of genuinely being loved through your artifice.

You tricked real feelings out of me and reveled in that. When you couldn't get that kick anymore, when the "new love scent" wore off this old jalopy, you traded me in for a newer model.

Foolish old man that I am, I believed in you, had faith in your love, and find myself only now able to extricate myself like the yolk from the white.

You and I can never have what we once dreamed of. What you did in broadcasting your lies and my private pain was inexcusable and a death blow. I can only hope that I send you on your way with a better perspective on who you are.

And maybe a few more views up your skirt.

But I doubt it. You're too scared to look into the abyss, the black hole. You blame Mike, you blame Jose and now you blame me for what you call the "manipulating the truth," when in point of fact, the truth had never been truer than when you heard it from me.

If only you had stopped wallowing in your own narcissistic self-pity long enough to listen, I should add.

You say you got a glimpse of what it was like for my wife, what it's like to live with me.

For the record, my wife is not an insane self-centered self-indulgent basket case of anxieties who takes pleasure in mocking people in order to grab a second's relief from her existence as a pathetic old hag.

She and I might have trouble communicating and the marriage is over, but at least, at LEAST she has the decency to treat me as her equal, a human being, as flawed as I am.

I see you clearly now. The thirty years that melted away when we met and made love were the facade of that pathetic old hag who has trapped the lover within you, the love that could have been.

Trapped her, because someone else hurt you badly. Learning to love means learning to get hurt because it is in the getting hurt that we learn what not to do, who not to be with. Protecting yourself against this, always running from the past crises, is to spite yourself. I committed the unforgivable sin of breaking through that facade, that protection, and making you lose control of yourself.

You said it: around me, you were speechless. It's when you're quiet that you've lost control of circumstances. You let go of the illusion you have that somehow you can keep everyone and everything in its place like table settings.

Like table settings, everything is neat and clean and orderly until the party starts: the silverware gets food on it, the napkins crumpled, the goblets get lip prints.

In other words people, especially lovers, are not for arranging. I am not to be arranged, controlled, managed, manipulated, pressured, hurt, punched, kicked, mocked, insulted, dangled, or smacked with lunchboxes!

Those thirty years that disappeared are back and form a permanent rictus over your face, an eternal death mask, plastered on with the careful panic of someone preventing a zombie attack by looking as dead as possible.

I mourn the death by asphyxiation of that marvelous young and beautiful woman.

So here we are, having completed a cosmic wheel back to our youth: you hate me, and I hate you.

I visited our bench every once in a while and sat on it, watched the seagulls fly up river and listened to the cars roll by. Nannies wheeled kids in strollers.

These could have been our grandkids.

Boys and girls, young people, rollerbladed and biked past and I thought about our children, the wonderful family we could have raised. Together.

Finally, I burned the bench after you went home from the now-somber reunion I arranged so carefully for you, for us. I could not bear the happy memories it held. They must be purged. Our hatred must be complete and utter.

Sometimes, I smile knowing that in an alternate universe somewhere, we're still sitting on that bench, grinning like two fools. Two blindly loving fools.

There, we are.

You are the common element in all your failures, in all those painful episodes. Take a good long look at yourself.

…and then go fuck off.

Made in the USA
Charleston, SC
17 March 2010